The sky over the Louvre

Invaded by the Europe of kings, plagued by the war in the Vendée and other revolts in Lyon and in Marseille, the Revolution is in dire straits. The people are famished, worried. The lines stretch in front of the shops, while the Public Safety Committee suspects everyone of counter-revolution. Three months before, Marat, the Friend of the People, was assassinated by Charlotte Corday. In a burst of patriotism, the painter David proposed to the Convention to do his posthumous portrait. And today, Robespierre is visiting his friend at his studio in the Louvre, in order to judge the state of the painting's progress.

BE HAPPY, MAXIMILIEN, I'VE WORKED FAST! THREE MONTHS TO GO, AT MOST.

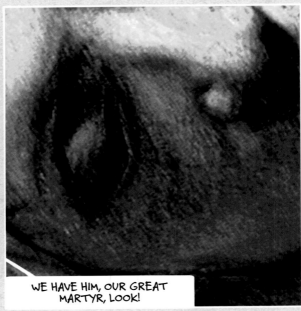

WE HAVE HIM, OUR GREAT MARTYR, LOOK!

HE'S NOT COMPLETELY DEAD YET. HE'S SIGHING HIS LAST BREATH.

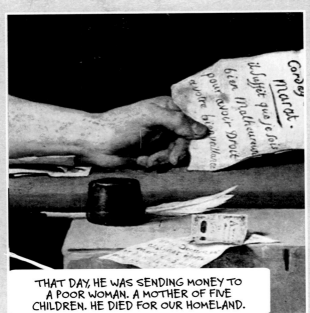

THAT DAY, HE WAS SENDING MONEY TO A POOR WOMAN. A MOTHER OF FIVE CHILDREN. HE DIED FOR OUR HOMELAND.

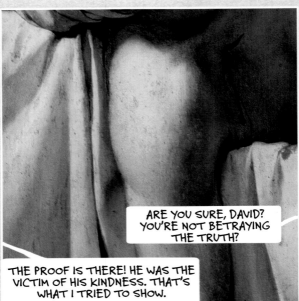

ARE YOU SURE, DAVID? YOU'RE NOT BETRAYING THE TRUTH?

THE PROOF IS THERE! HE WAS THE VICTIM OF HIS KINDNESS. THAT'S WHAT I TRIED TO SHOW.

LIKE JESUS ON THE CROSS, HIS HEAD IS BENT TO THE SIDE, A HALF-SMILE ON HIS LIPS. HE'S ALMOST BEAUTIFUL.

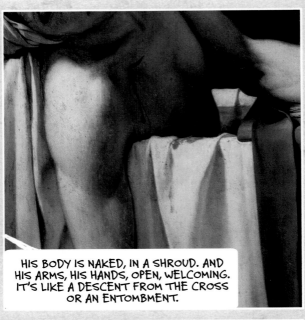

HIS BODY IS NAKED, IN A SHROUD. AND HIS ARMS, HIS HANDS, OPEN, WELCOMING. IT'S LIKE A DESCENT FROM THE CROSS OR AN ENTOMBMENT.

THE MORTAL WOUND, THERE, RECALLS THE SPEAR THRUST OF THE ROMAN SOLDIER. LIKEWISE FOR THE TRACES OF BLOOD ON THE WHITE SHEET. AND THE KNIFE, FALLEN ON THE GROUND. IT COULD BE ONE OF THE INSTRUMENTS OF THE PASSION.

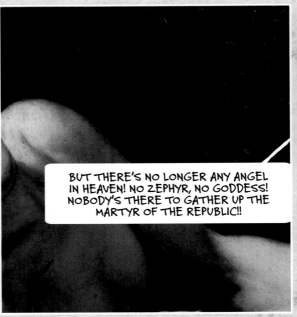

BUT THERE'S NO LONGER ANY ANGEL IN HEAVEN! NO ZEPHYR, NO GODDESS! NOBODY'S THERE TO GATHER UP THE MARTYR OF THE REPUBLIC!!

THE NEW HEAVEN IS EMPTY, MAXIMILIEN.

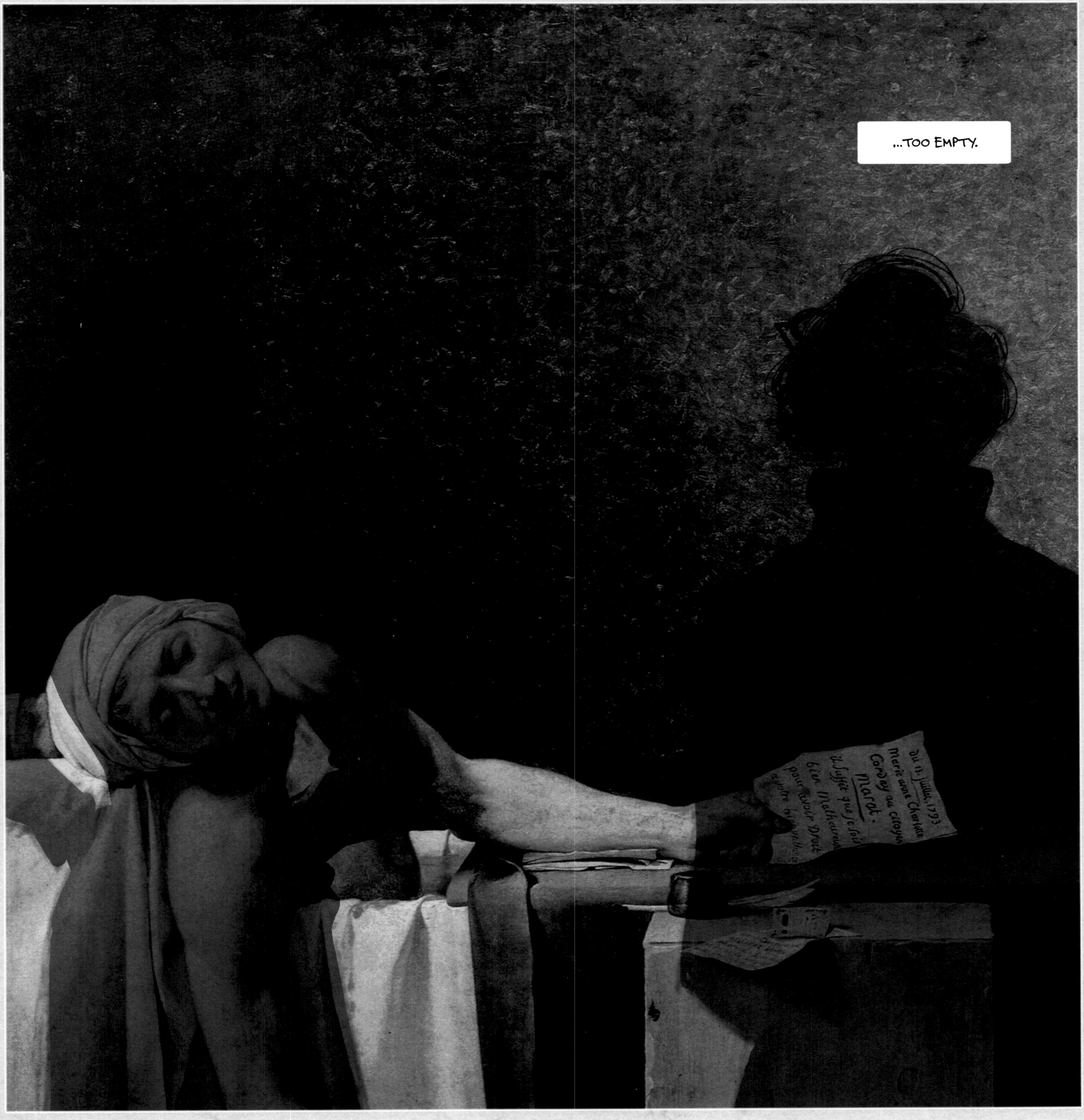
...TOO EMPTY.
Du 13. juillet. 1793
Marie anne Charlotte
Corday au citoyen
Marat.
il suffit que je sois
bien malheureuse
pour avoir Droit

Based on an idea by   Bernar Yslaire
Script, text, and dialogue   Jean-Claude Carrière and Bernar Yslaire
Production, drawing and coloring   Bernar Yslaire

Documentation assistant   Vincent Mezil
Paintings   Jacques-Louis David, Anne Louis Girodet,
Jean-Honoré Fragonard, Jean-Germain Drouais

Layout   Bernar Yslaire

Acknowledgments   Laurence Erlich, Fabrice Douar,
Sébastien Gnaedig, Geoffrey Haurey-Clos,
Lina Propeck, and Éditions Gallimard.

ISBN 978-1-56163-602-0
Library of Congress Control Number: 2010943384
© Futuropolis / Musee du Louvre Editions 2009
© 2011 NBM for the English translation
Translation by Joe Johnson
Lettering by Ortho
Printed in China
1st printing February 2011

The sky over the Louvre

Bernar YSLAIRE • Jean-Claude CARRIERE

Louvre

MUSÉE DU
LOUVRE
ÉDITIONS

NBM
ComicsLit

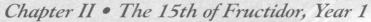

At the beginning of the month of August 1793, an unknown young man arrives in Paris. He's blond and speaks with a strong Slavic accent. He says his name is Jules Stern and that he comes from Khazaria, an old empire on the shores of the Black Sea. But nobody knows of Khazaria.

THE FALL OF THE BASTILLE, FOR TWELVE SOUS.

THE DECAPITATION OF THE TYRANT, FOR FIFTEEN SOUS!

AND THIS ONE?

EQUALITY? TEN SOUS.

BUT FRATERNITY IS MORE EXPENSIVE, OF COURSE!

DID THE KINGS LIVE HERE?

YES. AT VERSAILLES AND HERE, AT THE TUILERIES. BUT IT'S THE PEOPLE'S HOUSE NOW!

...THE PEOPLE'S?

WELL, YES. WHERE DID YOU COME FROM, CUTIE? WHAT ARE YOU LOOKING FOR?

I'M LOOKING FOR MY MOTHER.

YOU'LL ONLY FIND MEN HERE. BUT IF I CAN TAKE HER PLACE...

I HAVE AN APPOINTMENT WITH THE PAINTER DAVID. HE HAS HIS STUDIO HERE, I WAS TOLD.

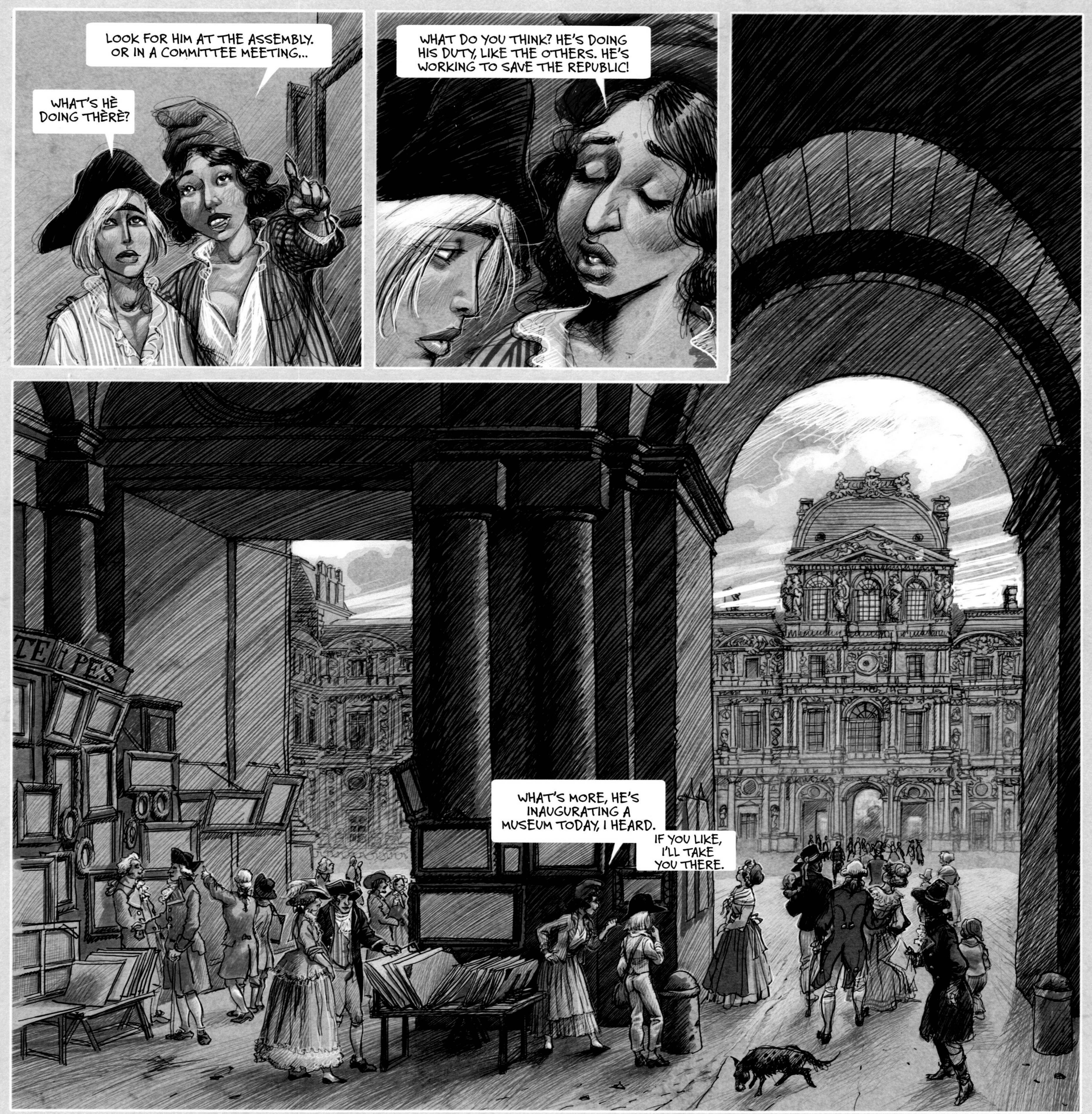
LOOK FOR HIM AT THE ASSEMBLY. OR IN A COMMITTEE MEETING...
WHAT'S HÈ DOING THÈRE?
WHAT DO YOU THINK? HE'S DOING HIS DUTY, LIKE THE OTHERS. HE'S WORKING TO SAVE THE REPUBLIC!
WHAT'S MORE, HE'S INAUGURATING A MUSEUM TODAY, I HEARD.
IF YOU LIKE, I'LL TAKE YOU THERE.

Chapter III: The 15th of Fructidor, Year 1

On the 8th of August 1793, the 15th of Fructidor of Year I, the Louvre is inaugurated as the first museum of the Nation. The date was carefully chosen: it's the anniversary of the official end of the monarchy a year earlier. It's also the first time that David crosses paths with Jules.

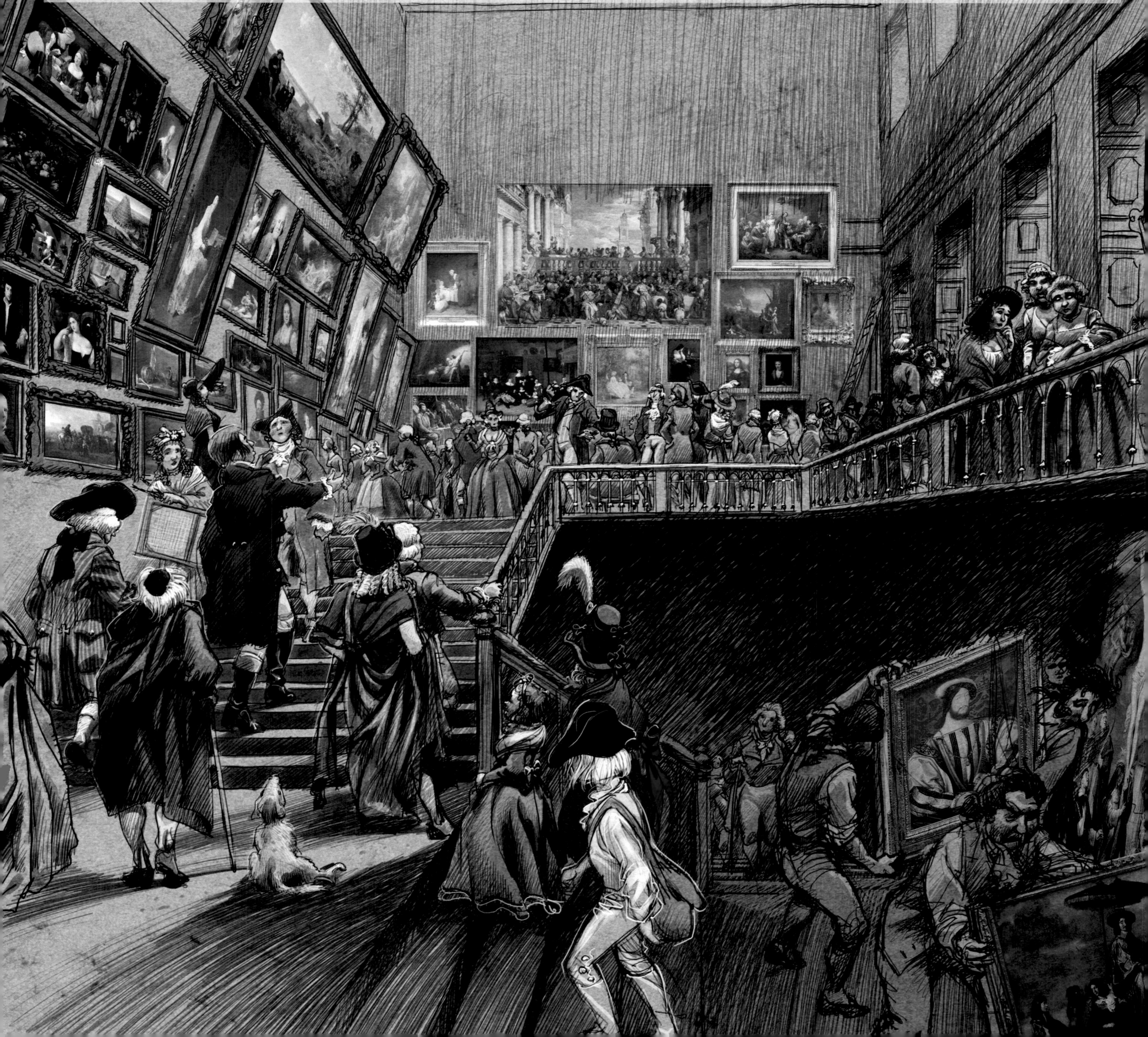

In the central Gallery, the portraits of banished kings and the religious subjects have already been taken down, sometimes even ripped down, then piled in the basements. The masterpieces of the *ancien régime* make way for the painters contemporary with the Revolution.

David, and his entire school: Drouais, Greuze, and Girodet, celebrate the beauty of the male body and the return to Antiquity. In that year of 1793, the unveiling of *The Sleep of Endymion*, brings glory to Girodet, acclaimed by critics and the public.

While the grandiloquent accents of the official speeches echo amid the antique sculptures, an old man wanders among the now-scorned, great French, Flemish, and Italian masters of the Renaissance. Jules is perhaps the only one to still recognize the painter Fragonard, still living in the Louvre.

x

14

OPENING A PUBLIC MUSEUM IS A REVOLUTIONARY DUTY!

IT'S PUTTING AT THE PEOPLE'S DISPOSAL THE WORKS OF ART USURPED BY THE FEW. IT'S OFFERING TO THE PEOPLE EXAMPLES OF PATRIOTISM AND VIRTUE.

IN THE ANCIENT RESIDENCE OF THE JUSTLY DEPOSED TYRANTS, AT A MOMENT WHEN OUR TROOPS ARE BATTLING VICTORIOUSLY AGAINST THE ENEMIES OF THE REVOLUTION, THERE NOW STANDS IN PLAIN LIGHT THE IDEAL IMAGES OF OUR NEW TIMES!

FOR THE REPUBLIC MUST DEFEND ITSELF WITH ARMS, BUT ALSO WITH IDEAS, WITH IMAGES, WITH SYMBOLS... WITH BEAUTY!!

YES, ART MUST BE ON OUR SIDE. IT MUST SET GREAT EXAMPLES. WE MUST ESTABLISH HERE A HERITAGE OF LIBERTY!!

WHØ'S SPÈAKING?

WHAT? WHY THAT'S ROBESPIERRE!

AND THE FAT ONE WITH THICK LIPS IS DANTON! AH! YOU SHOULD HEAR HIM SPEAK!

AND DAVID? WHICH ØNÈ IS HÈ?

HE'S THE ONE WITH THE SWOLLEN CHEEK. HEY, HE'S GOING TO SPEAK. THAT'S HIM.

UNDER THE HATED REGIME THAT WE'VE ABOLISHED, THE MAJORITY OF FRENCH ARTISTS PROSTITUTED AND DISHONORED THEMSELVES. THEY HAVE CENTURIES OF DEBASEMENT TO ERASE!!

THE EFFEMINATE BRUSHES OF BOUCHER AND VANLOO COULDN'T INSPIRE THAT VIGOROUS, MALE STYLE WHICH MUST CHARACTERIZE REVOLUTIONARY EXPLOITS.

TO PAINT THE ENERGY OF A PEOPLE THAT HAS BURST FROM THE BONDS OF HUMAN KIND, WE MUST HAVE PROUD COLORS, A VIGOROUS STYLE, A BOLD BRUSH, A VOLCANIC GENIUS!!

The Public Safety Committee has the task of naming suspects. The Committee seeks them out and sends the accused before the Revolutionary Tribunal. It composes the arrest orders, which was are carried out under the direction of twelve policemen from Paris named by the Commune. As a fervent patriot, David sits on the committee. He's not expecting to meet Jules there once again.

THEY HELPED YOU, AND YOU PUT THEM ON YOUR LIST?

IF THEY'RE ENEMIES OF THE REVOLUTION, WHY NOT? IT'S UP TO THE TRIBUNAL TO JUDGE, CITIZEN LE BAS.

ON THE OTHER HAND, THAT MADAME TRUDAINE WHOM YOU'RE TO PAINT. THEY SAY SHE WAS A FRIEND OF ONE OF THE AUSTRIAN WOMAN'S SERVANTS.

WITH NO PROOF, FOR THE MOMENT.

CITIZENS, THERE'S A BOY HERE WHO'D LIKE TO DENOUNCE SOMEONE, BUT ONLY TO CITIZEN DAVID.

HAVE HIM COME IN.

DO YOU KNOW HIM?

WHAT'S YOUR NAME?

JULÈS STÈRN.

WHOM DO WISH TO DENOUNCE?

MY MØTHÈR.

YOU'RE NOT THE FIRST. WHAT DID YOUR MOTHER DO?

SHÈ KILLÈD CITIZÈN MARAT.

ANOTHER LUNATIC! UNBELIEVABLE...

YOU'RE SPEAKING NONSENSE, MY BOY. MARAT WAS ASSASSINATED BY A WOMAN NAMED CHARLOTTE CORDAY. SHE DENOUNCED HERSELF. AND SHE WAS A VIRGIN.

JULES STERN... ARE YOU A JEW?

NOT EXACTLY. I COME FROM KHAZARIA, THE ONLY COUNTRY THAT EVER CONVERTED TO JUDAISM. WHY DO YOU ASK?

NO REASON. AND WHY DO YOU SAY YOUR MOTHER KILLED MARAT?

BECAUSE SHE'S KILLING EVERYONE. SHE'LL KILL YOU, TOO, CITIZEN ROBESPIERRE!

MINE DIED WHEN I WAS A CHILD, AND MY FATHER RAN AWAY, HE ABANDONED ME.

I'M A CHILD OF THE NATION. SHE IS MY TRUE MOTHER.

THAT'S JUST WHAT I WAS SAYING.

An uneasy silence follows Jules' words. But Robespierre pretends to have not heard.
While the young boy is led away by the guards, the Incorruptible fixedly observes him leaving. David sets his hand on his shoulder, as though to soothe him.
"Let him go; he's only thirteen. At that age you don't know what you're saying. You're young, handsome, and innocent. Like an angel…"
"I don't know anyone who's innocent," responds Robespierre.

Chapter V: The 28th of Brumaire, Year II

It's evening time at the Duplays' home. The Incorruptible has made his quarters there and receives his loyal supporters in the grand salon. David, Saint-Just, Couthon, Le Bas, and Bonbon, Maximilien's brother, are there. The dinner is frugal. As usual, Madame Duplay, who loves to spoil her prestigious guest, has saved a large platter of fresh oranges just for him. The acidity of the orange juice has the rare quality of soothing the Jacobin's uneasy stomach. A part of the evening is spent in dutifully peeling them, all the while commenting on the grand theme that seems to have been preoccupying Robespierre for some time. Saint-Just doesn't hide his incredulity. As soon as it concerns politics, David doesn't say much. He draws…

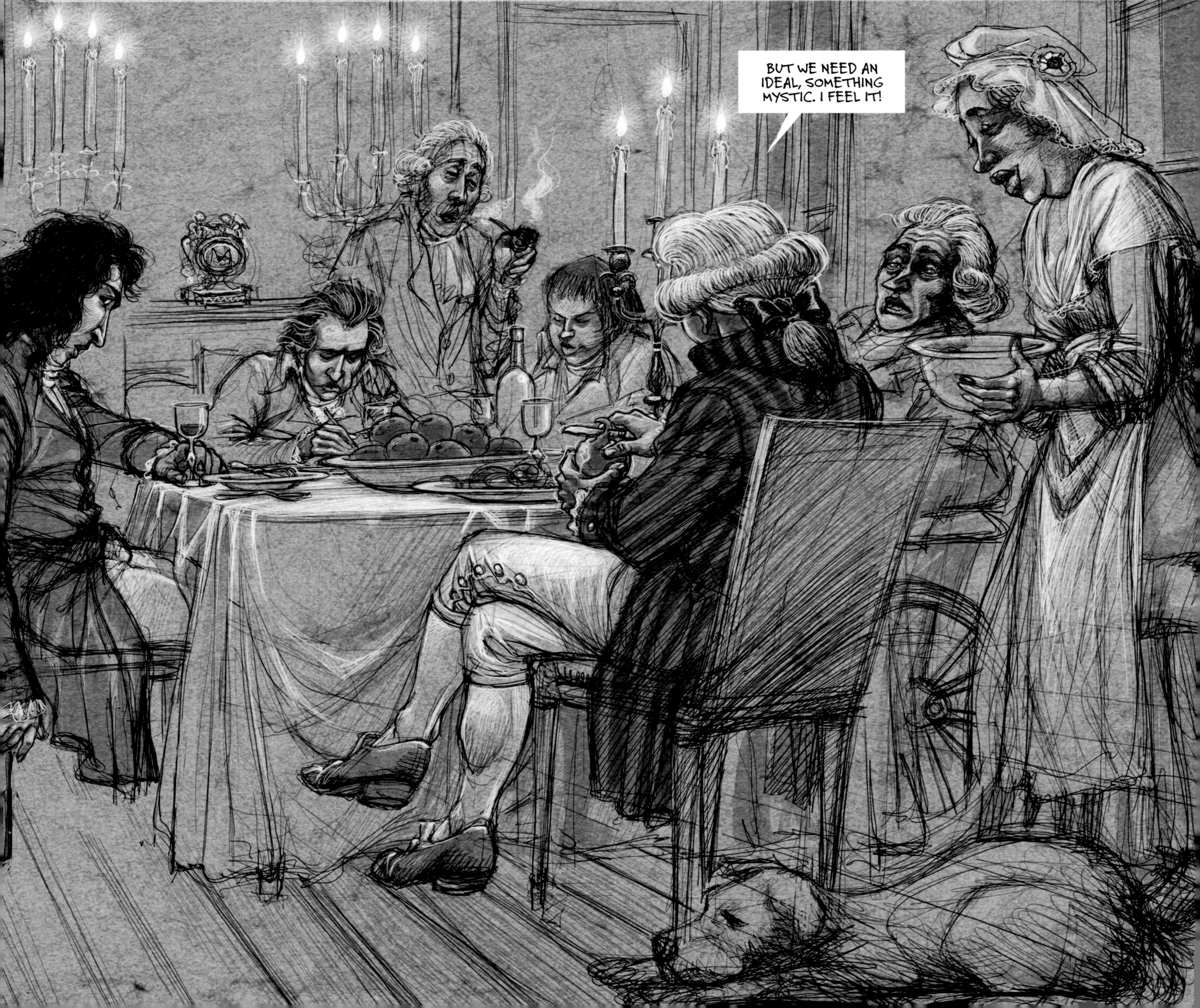
BUT WE NEED AN IDEAL, SOMETHING MYSTIC. I FEEL IT!

WE CANNOT EMPTY HEAVEN!

IT EMPTIED ITSELF ON ITS OWN!

YOU SURELY DON'T WANT TO PUT GOD BACK IN? THE PEOPLE WOULDN'T UNDERSTAND. IT WOULD SMACK OF A RETURN TO SUPERSTITION.

BUT HOW TO HOLD ON TO A PEOPLE WITHOUT A FAITH? WITHOUT AN AFTERLIFE? WITHOUT SOMETHING ELSE?

WITH LAWS, MAXIMILIEN. LAWS ARE THE POPULAR WILL.

THE LAW ISN'T ENOUGH, SAINT-JUST. WE SHOULD TOLERATE A PURIFIED RELIGION. AND RECOGNIZE THE FREEDOM OF WORSHIP.

AT WHAT COST! IT WOULD BE A SIGN OF WEAKNESS! THE CHURCH HAS ALWAYS TAKEN THE SIDE OF DESPOTS. IT WOULD REAR ITS HEAD AGAIN.

WHAT THEN?

I PROPOSE THAT WE ORGANIZE A GREAT FESTIVAL OF REASON!

OF REASON?

OF REASON, YES! THAT'S OUR NEW GOD! THAT'S WHAT WE SHOULD CELEBRATE! AND WHY NOT IN NOTRE DAME? IN THE FORMER CATHEDRAL?

A FESTIVAL OF REASON? YES, PERHAPS...OR MAYBE OF THE ETERNAL? OF THE UNIVERSAL SOUL? HOW TO EXPRESS IT?

DAVID, YOU DON'T HAVE AN IDEA?

PARDON ME, MAXIMILIEN, BUT THERE'S A DISPATCH HERE THAT'S JUST ARRIVED.

DEFECTIONS IN BORDEAUX...AND OTHER UPRISINGS IN CALVADOS.

YES, YES, I KNOW. EXCUSE ME. I'M SO TIRED.

WHERE ARE THE SOLDIERS TO BE FOUND? THE MONEY? CAN WE ASK FOR FURTHER SACRIFICES?

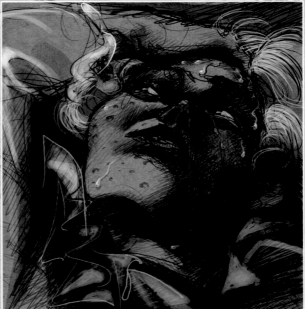

In order to preserve the Revolution's conquests at all costs, in September 1793, the Convention decrees "Terror to be the order of the day." The ex-queen Marie Antoinette, renamed Citizeness Capet, is one of the first victims.

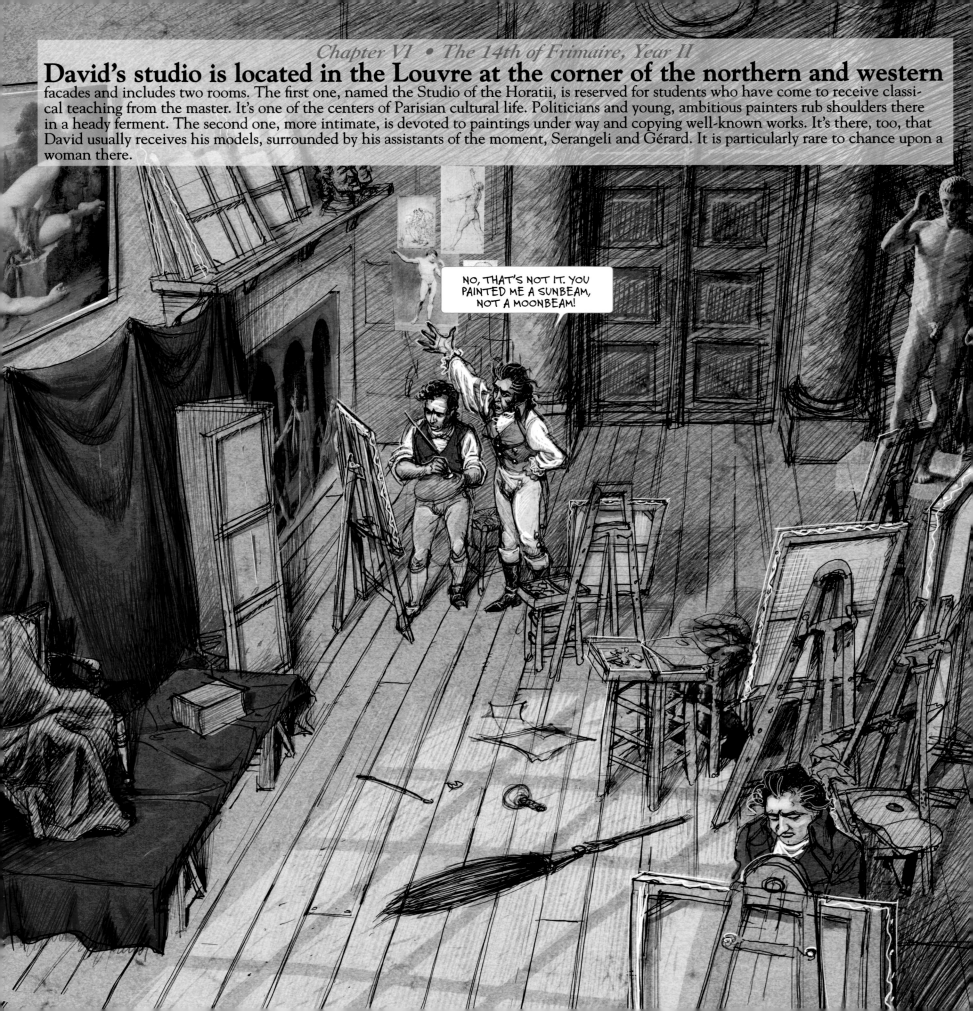

David's studio is located in the Louvre at the corner of the northern and western facades and includes two rooms. The first one, named the Studio of the Horatii, is reserved for students who have come to receive classical teaching from the master. It's one of the centers of Parisian cultural life. Politicians and young, ambitious painters rub shoulders there in a heady ferment. The second one, more intimate, is devoted to paintings under way and copying well-known works. It's there, too, that David usually receives his models, surrounded by his assistants of the moment, Serangeli and Gérard. It is particularly rare to chance upon a woman there.

I DON'T SEE HOW HE DID IT... THE LIGHT, I MEAN.

I DON'T HAVE TIME TO EXPLAIN TO YOU. MONSIEUR GIRODET PREFERS TO REMAIN IN ROME. GO ASK HIM, IF YOU LIKE.

TELL ME, GÉRARD...THE BLOND BOY WHO WANTED TO SEE ME, THE ONE WHO LOOKS LIKE AN ANGEL... HAS ANYONE SEEN HIM AGAIN?

HE MUST HAVE FLOWN AWAY.

AH! CITIZENESS TRUDAINE! COME IN, SIT DOWN.

WELL? MY PORTRAIT?

HERE IT IS. ALMOST FINISHED.

FINISHED? BUT...WE'D AGREED ON SOME FURNITURE, A WINDOW, A GARDEN...

THAT'S ALL OLD-FASHIONED, CITIZENESS. ACADEMIC CONVENTION...

THE TIMES CHANGE. EVERYTHING'S ON THE MOVE, PAINTING, TOO!

THAT'S TRUE, EVERYTHING'S GOING SO FAST. OUR LEADERS ARE DISAPPEARING ONE AFTER THE OTHER. IS THIS TERROR GOING TO LAST A LONG TIME?

AS LONG AS NECESSARY.

WHERE ARE WE HEADING? DO YOU KNOW?

WE'RE HEADING TOWARDS LIBERTY AND EQUALITY, CITIZENESS. TOWARDS A BETTER SOCIETY...AND EQUAL FOR EVERYONE...LIKE THAT SCUMBLE THERE, BEHIND YOU, DO YOU UNDERSTAND?

YES, THAT'S WHERE WE'RE HEADING. IF I PAINT FOR YOU A CHEST OF DRAWERS OR A GARDEN, I DISTINGUISH YOU FROM OTHERS; IT'S LIKE A PRIVILEGE.

YES, I UNDERSTAND, I UNDERSTAND.

AH, BY THE WAY...I BROUGHT YOU WHAT I OWE YOU.

YES, YES. THANK YOU. GO SIT DOWN, FOR THE FINAL TOUCH UPS.

WHO KNOWS IF I COULD STILL BE PAINTED TOMORROW?

WHO KNOWS IF I'LL STILL BE ABLE TO COME WITH MY HEAD ON MY SHOULDERS.

YES...WHO KNOWS?

AND YOU, TOO... ALL OF YOU...

At the Club of the Cordeliers, Danton and Robespierre are facing off. The subject they're debating divides them more than the Terror does. The question is an ideological one for the Montagnards.

AND PERHAPS PUT A PHRYGIAN CAP ON HIM? HAVE HIM SING "THE CARMAGNOLE"?

I WANT WHAT THE PEOPLE WANT. WHAT THEY NEED.

TOO BAD GOD DOESN'T HAVE A HEAD! WE KNOW FULL WELL WHAT WE'D DO WITH IT!

AND TO SAY THAT THE PEOPLE RECOGNIZE THEMSELVES IN HIM!

DO YOU FIND HIM VULGAR?

WORSE! THE VERY FACE OF CORRUPTION.

Later, when the meeting ends, Robespierre takes David aside. The polemic launched by Danton spawned a sterile debate, which stirred up the assembly of Jacobins. But the Incorruptible, as usual, doesn't become flustered and reflects out loud. He comes back to his obsession.

At the National Convention, they learn of the death of a brave thirteen-year-old. Beneath the posthumous portraits of Le Peletier and Marat, both assassinated, a uniformed general reads the dispatch that relates the heroic deeds of the new martyr. In the galleries, the delegates' emotions run very high.

I THINK YOU'VE READ INCORRECTLY, GENERAL.

I'LL START OVER...SURROUNDED BY BANDITS WHO THREATENED HIM WITH DEATH ON THE ONE HAND AND ON THE OTHER DEMANDED THAT HE CRY "LONG LIVE THE KING!" HE PAID WITH HIS LIFE FOR HAVING CRIED OUT "LONG LIVE THE REPUBLIC!"

THIS YOUNG MARTYR SUPPORTED HIS MOTHER THROUGH HIS LABOR. IT'S NOT POSSIBLE TO CHOOSE A MORE BEAUTIFUL EXAMPLE OF VIRTUE!! ONLY THE FRENCH HAVE THIRTEEN-YEAR-OLD HEROES!

FOR THE YOUNG BARA, I PROPOSE A CEREMONY WORTHY OF HIS DEATH!! AND THE HONORS OF THE PANTHEON!!

THAT CHILD, THAT MARTYR MUST HAVE HIS IMAGE PAINTED BY THE BRUSHES OF THE ILLUSTRIOUS DAVID!!

DAVID, IT'S FOR YOU TO IMMORTALIZE THE YOUNG BARA DYING FOR THE REPUBLIC!

MAY HE TAKE HIS PLACE HERE, AT THIS ASSEMBLY, BETWEEN MARAT AND LE PELETIER!

YES, DAVID! DO HIS PORTRAIT FOR US, WHICH WE'LL ENGRAVE, SO IT WILL MAKE THE ROUNDS IN SCHOOLS!

I ACCEPT, FOR THOSE ARE THE DEEDS THAT I LOVE TO DEPICT!

They'll speak no further of it for several weeks.

The end of February, David's studio is closed to the public. In his own words,
David needs to gather himself in order to reach the sublime. The portrait of the Supreme Being demands it of him. To do so, he surrounds himself only with the young Gérard and his usual assistant, Serangeli. The latter has recruited a few models in the nearby Tuileries gardens.

TOO RUSTIC, A TRUE PEASANT.

NO. TOO STOOPED, TOO SICKLY... YOU CAN SEE HIS RIBS.

TOO LIMP, THAT ONE, HIS SHOULDERS FALL!

YOU WANTED A YOUNG BOY. WHAT EXACTLY ARE YOU LOOKING FOR?

I DON'T KNOW! BUT A VIRILE BEAUTY IN ANY CASE! AND YOUNG, YES! LIKE THE HOPE FOR A NEW WORLD!

AND LOOK AT WHAT YOU BRING ME! THIS ONE HAS AN EYE HIGHER THAN THE OTHER!

I NEED HARMONY, YOU UNDERSTAND? SYMMETRY!

WHAT?

YOU THINK TOO HIGHLY OF SYMMETRY, DAVID.

TOO MUCH RIGOR, TOO MUCH BALANCE DETRACT FROM HARMONY, YOU KNOW.

BE QUIET, FRAGONARD! AND LOOK AT YOU! WHAT DO YOU UNDERSTAND ABOUT OUR TIMES? WHAT DO YOU UNDERSTAND ABOUT THE BEAUTY OF ANTIQUITY?

YOU'RE RIGHT. I'M NO DOUBT TOO OLD TO CONTINUE TO PAINT.

COME IN, HE'S WAITING FOR YOU. YOUR TIME HAS COME.

"Come closer," says David. "Yes, closer! And get undressed."

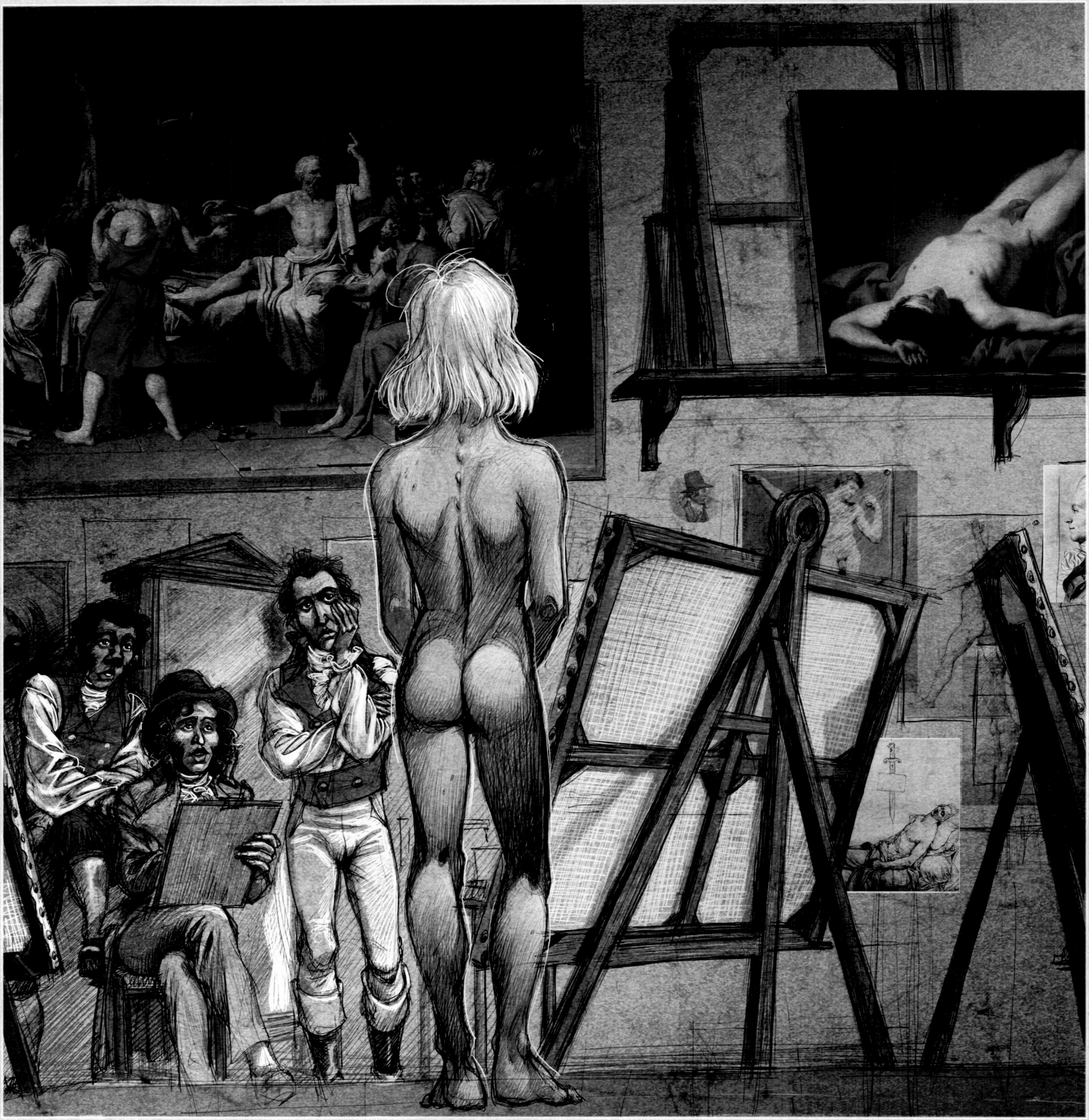

THE REPUBLIC IS ORDERING AN IMAGE OF VIRTUE FROM ME. I MUST PAINT THE SUPREME BEING.

WHAT DOES THAT MEAN?

I HAVEN'T THE FAINTEST. THAT WHICH GOES BEYOND US, NO DOUBT, WHAT TRANSCENDS US. ACCORDING TO ROBESPIERRE, HIS CULT MUST GIVE RISE TO A VIRTUOUS SOCIETY, A NEW MAN.

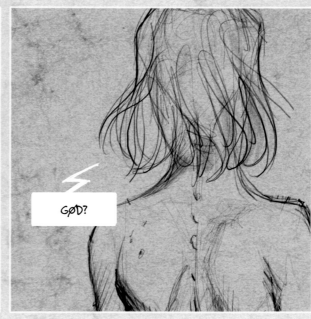

GOD?

NO! ESPECIALLY NOT GOD!! THE REPUBLIC HAS BANISHED THE CHALICE AND THE MONSTRANCE, AND THE PEOPLE NEED A NEW IDEAL, CLOSER TO THEM, MORE SINCERE... THE SUPREME BEING!!

BUT BY DEFINITION, THE BEING HAS NO APPEARANCE, NO IMAGE.

I KNOW. IT'S ROBESPIERRE'S IDEA. BUT AFTER ALL, IT'S THE GENIUS OF EVERY GREAT PAINTER TO GIVE SHAPE TO THE INVISIBLE!

BUT HOW ARE YOU GOING TO REPRESENT HIM? IS HE BLOND, BRUNETTE? HOW OLD IS HE? IS IT A WOMAN? IS IT A MAN?

FOR ME, IT COULD BE A THIRTEEN-YEAR-OLD BOY..AND WHY NOT ANDROGYNOUS? WHAT DO YOU THINK ABOUT THAT?

IN ANY CASE, FEMALE MODELS ARE FORBIDDEN IN THE STUDIO. RIGHT, GÉRARD?

YES, WOMEN LACK SYMMETRY. THEY HAVE TOO MANY LUMPS.

A month later, David's work hasn't advanced very much. Sketches litter the studio's floor. Jules is still there. Patiently, he follows David's intuitions as best he can. Between the painter and his model, little by little, a complicity is established.

YÈS.

AH? WELL?

SHÈ DIDN'T RÈCØGNIZE MÈ. NØT YÈT. SHÈ'S TØØ BUSY DÈVØURING HÈR ØWN CHILDRÈN. ALSO...

YES?

I HAVÈN'T FINISHÈD MY MISSIØN.

WHAT MISSION? A SECRET MISSION?

YØUR STUDÈNTS DISTRUST MÈ.

RØBÈSPIÈRRÈ, TØØ. HÈ DØÈSN'T LIKE MÈ.

HE TOLD YOU SO?

I GUÈSS IT. THÈ SUPRÈMÈ BÈING CAN BE NØNÈ THÈR THAN HIMSÈLF. HÈ HAS AN IDØL'S AMBITIØN.

I FORBID YOU TO SAY THAT!

RESUME YOUR POSE AND SHUT UP!! SHUT UP!!

Maximilien de Robespierre is stylish. Every morning, his personal hairdresser visits him at the Duplays', following behind Doctor Soubielle. The former cares for his outward appearance, whereas the latter cares for his internal organs. It's also the occasion to take stock of the coming day in the company of his loyal supporters.

WHY NOT? NOBODY KNOWS HIS FACE! AND WE NEED AN IDEAL FIGURE! THAT'S UNIDENTIFIABLE! THE TWO OF THEM ARE JUMBLED FOR ME.

I DIDN'T PICTURE THE SUPREME BEING AS A YOUNG MARTYR FOR THE REPUBLIC, BUT LIKE THE UNIVERSAL FATHER RATHER.

AND I SEE HIM AS HIS SON, HANDSOME LIKE AN IDEAL OF ANTIQUITY, RECEIVING IN HIS FINAL BREATH THE REVELATION OF THE EXISTENCE OF THAT BEING...

...BUT ONLY HIS GAZE TURNED TOWARDS THE SKY ATTESTS TO IT... THE EYE OF REPUBLICAN CONSCIENCE!!

MMH...AND YET, ONE CANNOT REPLACE THE OTHER. NO, WE MUST HAVE TWO, QUITE DISTINCT FESTIVALS!!

AND TWO PORTRAITS! BUT PERHAPS YOU HAVEN'T YET FOUND A MODEL FOR THE FIRST? SEARCH! SEARCH MORE, DAVID!

DO YOU REMEMBER THAT BOY WHO CAME FROM KHAZARIA?

WASN'T HE JEWISH?

YES, BUT IN FACT, THEY'RE A CONVERTED PEOPLE. THERE'S NOTHING SEMITIC ABOUT THEM.

ALL THE SAME: JESUS WAS A JEW. SOME MIGHT SEE TOO DIRECT OF AN ALLUSION THEREIN.

NO, NO, FIND ME SOMEONE ELSE. THE SUPREME BEING IS BEYOND GOD, YOU UNDERSTAND?

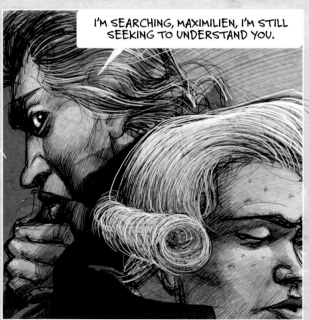

I'M SEARCHING, MAXIMILIEN, I'M STILL SEEKING TO UNDERSTAND YOU.

In the spring, the pose has evolved. The Supreme Being lies on the ground now, and is confused with Bara, the martyr of the Revolution. Pressing a Revolutionary cockade on his chest, Jules is supposed to look through the studio's window at the sky over the Louvre. David has regained his inspiration.

Elsewhere, in an office of the General Security, Gérard speaks to a secretary.

The latter is taking down dictation from a woman. A large poster of the Declaration of the Rights of Man adorns the flaking walls.

Grabbing a small notebook, David's assistant says quietly:

"I've come to bring the names of several potential enemies of the Nation. First, there's a young foreigner…"

The secretary interrupts him with a gesture:

"One moment. This citizeness is first. And then all those there, who are waiting for their turn."

The assistant turns around. He sees a good fifteen people, men and women, seated or standing. They're all holding a piece of paper or a notebook in their hands, and await their turn to denounce someone.

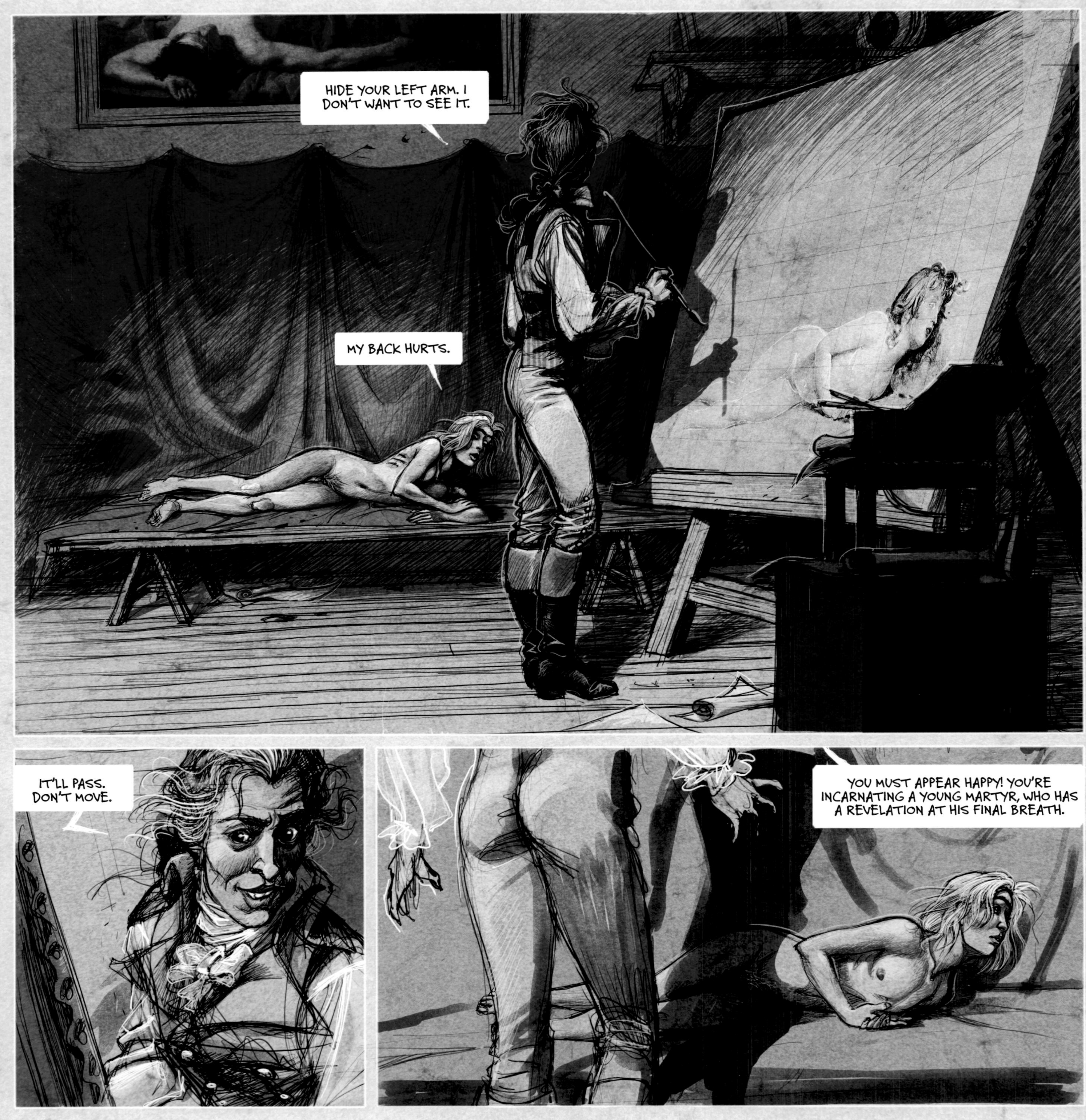
HIDE YOUR LEFT ARM. I DON'T WANT TO SEE IT.
MY BACK HURTS.
IT'LL PASS. DON'T MOVE.
YOU MUST APPEAR HAPPY! YOU'RE INCARNATING A YOUNG MARTYR, WHO HAS A REVELATION AT HIS FINAL BREATH.

ESPECIALLY DON'T MOVE! LIFT YOUR EYES TOWARDS THE HEIGHTS, TOWARDS THE SUMMITS.

LOOK TOWARDS THE SKY. YOU SEE THE BEYOND.

I DON'T SEE ANYTHING IN THE SKY.

THEN GO AWAY! GET THE HELL OUT!! I'LL DO IT WITHOUT YOU.

In the spring, Danton and his friends are arrested and led before the
Revolutionary Tribunal. Six days after the execution of Hébert the Enraged, it's the Indulgents' turn to be accused of conspiring against the Republic and condemned to the guillotine. When Danton passes in his cart before the Duplays' house where Robespierre lives, he cries out: "You'll follow me soon enough!" But the Incorruptible doesn't hear, entirely occupied as he is in preparing his grand festival of the spring with David.

AND THE SEQUENCE OF THE FESTIVAL?

THE PARADE WILL START WITH THREE BONFIRES IN THE TUILERIES GARDENS.

WE'LL BURN STATUES THERE OF TYRANNY, SUPERSTITION, AND SELFISHNESS.

AND ATHEISM. ATHEISM MUST BE BURNT, TOO.

I THOUGHT OF A STATUE WRAPPED IN OAKUM. AFTER BURNING, IT WOULD LET WISDOM APPEAR.

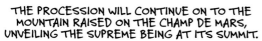

THE PROCESSION WILL CONTINUE ON TO THE MOUNTAIN RAISED ON THE CHAMP DE MARS, UNVEILING THE SUPREME BEING AT ITS SUMMIT.

A SCULPTOR MUST MAKE A STATUE OF IT THAT WILL OVERLOOK THE CAPITAL.

I'D ORDERED A PORTRAIT FROM YOU, TO MAKE ENGRAVINGS OF IT AND CONTRIBUTE TO THE EDIFICATION OF THE PEOPLE. HAVE YOU FORGOTTEN?

ON THE CONTRARY, MAXIMILIEN, I'M WORKING ON IT! I'M WORKING ON IT! I SPEND ALL MY NIGHTS ON IT.

SOME HAVE REPORTED TO ME THAT YOU WERE LABORING AWAY AT THE ONE OF BARA?

SLANDER! I SPEND MY NIGHTS PAINTING THE SUPREME IDEAL! BUT I CONFESS TO YOU, ROBESPIERRE, IT'S THE VISION OF DAVID! I'LL DO NOTHING DETRIMENTAL TO MY GLORY!!

47

IT'S ALSO BEEN REPORT-ED TO ME THAT YOU'VE KEPT THAT YOUNG JEW ON AS A MODEL...I'D FORBIDDEN YOU TO DO SO.

THAT'S FALSE. I GOT RID OF HIM!

YOU DON'T BELIEVE ME? DO YOU DISTRUST ME?

IN ANY CASE, HE'S BEEN ARRESTED.

"*Arrested?*" cries out David, dumbfounded. "*But why?*"
"*He was seen at Danton's. He was still seeking his mother.*"
"*He's going to find his widow,*" says Couthon.
David gets up and quickly leaves the studio, crying out:
"*I must find him!*"
The others watch him leave without understanding.

At the Conciergerie, the condemned await with anguish the call of the people's

commissioner designating them for the next trip. Thereupon follows the ritual where the hair upon their neck is cut to facilitate the guillotine's blade. There are defrocked priests, aristocrats or unjustly accused victims there thronging together before the departure of the final cart. David plunges through the crowd with authority and heads towards the citizen guard holding the day's list. While the latter calls out the names of the future spouses of the Widow (as the Guillotine became known), the painter scans the crowd and shivers.
From the cold, no doubt. He doesn't see Jules anywhere.
From the back of the room, a voice calls to him:
"*David! David, help me! Do you recognize me? Have Pity! I'm innocent! David!*"
It's Madame Trudaine.
For as instant, the painter focuses on this woman who's begging him, then his hurried gaze turns towards the guard, and he asks him:
"*Blond, young, very handsome...Do you recognize him?*" he says while showing him two sketches of Jules.
"*I think he left this morning,*" the sans-culotte answers gruffly.
"*Left where?*"
"*Where do you think people go when they leave here?*" asked the other, laughing.
In the back of the room, two guards are already leading away Madame Trudaine.

The Place de la Révolution is packed. The Idol of the people is executed around five in the evening. When Danton steps up to the guillotine, he says to the executioner: "Hold up my head to the people. It's worth the show." Which is done… Resigned, Camille Desmoulins follows him. Jules is behind him. Jostling the crowd while passing through and brushing aside the knitting-women, David arrives at the foot of the guillotine at the moment when Sanson pushes the young boy.

Night has fallen on the Place de la Révolution. A tarpaulin now covers the guillotine and flaps in the wind. Two shabbily dressed workers, equipped with wooden buckets, are cleaning the base of the machine with rags and brushes. Not far from there, some soldiers are warming themselves around a fire, and stray dogs lap at the traces of blood. David shows his Conventioneer papers to the soldiers:

"Tell me, where are the bodies carried to?"

"To the Errancis Cemetery, like all the others."

"And the heads?"

"The heads, too, no doubt."

The Errancis Cemetery is used for the recently guillotined. From Year 1 of the Republic until the final days of Thermidor, the majority of the great heads of the Revolution, along with their bodies, are thrown into communal graves. They're covered with quicklime so that the subsequent generations won't ever be able to recognize the traitors. Indulgents and Girondists, Hébertistes and the Enraged Ones, all share the same grave. The Republic that they created offers them all equality in death.

The Incorruptible hasn't appeared at the Assembly in a month. He's said to be

weakened, for neither his enemies nor his illness leave him the slightest respite. During his public absence, never has the Terror claimed so many victims, whereas he himself spits blood every night, and puts himself in the care of Éléonore Duplay and her mother.

SOME PEOPLE SPEND THE ENTIRE NIGHT IN COACHES, FOR FEAR OF RETURNING HOME. AND NOW, WHEN THE CART PASSES, PEOPLE CLOSE THEIR WINDOWS INSTEAD OF APPLAUDING.

THE OTHER DAY, I SAW THE WORD *CANNIBALS* WRITTEN IN BIG LETTERS ON A WALL. THE PEOPLE ARE SUFFERING, THAT'S FOR SURE.

ARE WE BLOODTHIRSTY MONSTERS?

SETTLE DOWN, CLOSE YOUR EYES. YOU MUST GET WELL. AND RETURN TO THE ASSEMBLY.

WHAT IMAGE WILL REMAIN OF US? HOW WILL THE MEN OF TOMORROW JUDGE US?

I DON'T LOVE BLOOD...THE SMELL, THE SIGHT OF BLOOD...SPILLING IT DISGUSTS ME... ALWAYS HAS.

REST EASY, THE WAR IN THE VENDÉE IS SETTLING DOWN. THE CHOUANS HAVE WITHDRAWN FROM GRANVILLE.

EVEN THE ENEMIES FROM OUTSIDE ARE PULLING BACK!

DO YOU BELIEVE THAT THE TERROR IS STILL NECESSARY?

EVERYONE'S WONDERING.

Between April and July 1794, 2,100 heads fall in Paris.

It's a historic vote at the Convention. The Incorruptible takes the platform, simultaneously pale and triumphant, more powdered than ever. He proposes the adoption of a new decree. In the Assembly, docile hands are raised. Some delegates are asleep in their seats, others are trying to clean their boots, like someone washing their hands, hoping to wipe off the blood that has splattered their shoes. In the galleries, there is murmuring. The Terror has created a conspiracy of fear.

I PROPOSE THAT WE ADOPT THE FOLLOWING DECREE: ARTICLE ONE, THE FRENCH PEOPLE RECOGNIZE THE EXISTENCE OF THE SUPREME BEING AND THE IMMORTALITY OF THE SOUL.

ARTICLE TWO: THE PEOPLE RECOGNIZE THAT THE CULT OF THE SUPREME BEING IS THE PRACTICE OF MAN'S DUTIES. ARTICLE THREE: THE PEOPLE PLACE FOREMOST AMONG THESE DUTIES TO DESPISE BAD FAITH, TO FLEE THE TYRANNY OF TRAITORS, TO SUCCOR THE WRETCHED, TO RESPECT THE WEAK...

I KNOW WHO THE SUPREME BEING IS...

ME, TOO, BUT I'M NOT SURE HE'S IMMORTAL.

The speech is barely over before obedient hands are raised. The decree is adopted unanimously. And the date of the Festival of the Supreme Being is set for the 20th of Prairial, Year II, a month later. Everyone sees in it Robespierre's triumph.

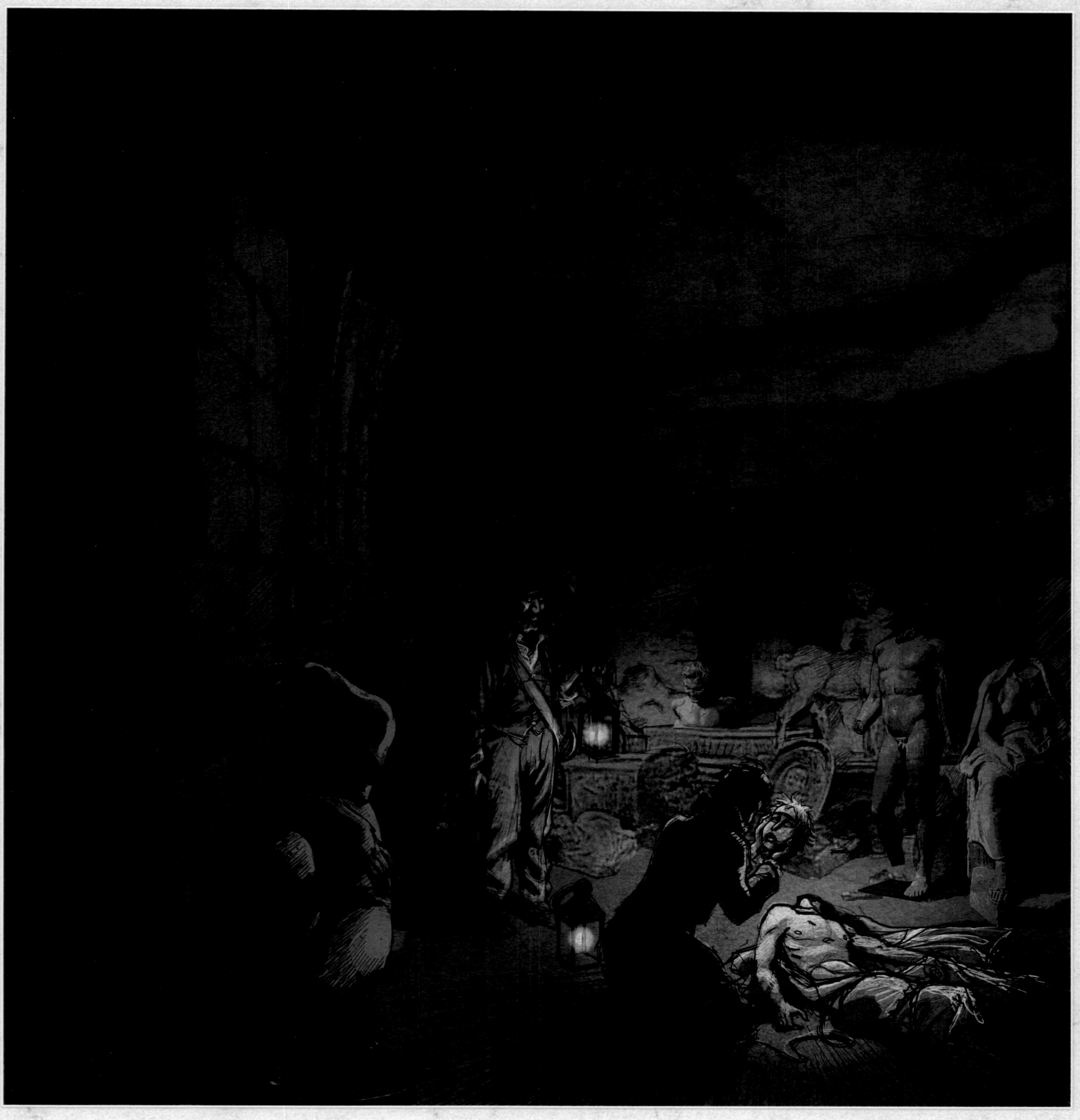

The night of that same day, in a basement of the Louvre cluttered with rejected
and broken religious statues, David is alone, facing Jules' separated head set on a white sheet. He draws this dead head tirelessly by the
glow of lanterns, with a scarf knotted over his face. Several rejected sketches litter the floor. One of his assistants stands at a distance.
The sans-culotte paid by David holds a lantern that lights the scene. He can be seen laying down Jules' body, wrapped in a large canvas. Each one has a go at matching up the torso and head, stitching them back together, and making use of pulleys and winches. There's
something of Dr. Frankenstein's laboratory about it.

Ghostlike, Fragonard passes by the back of the room, watching the dawning of Modern Times.

And David's assistant whispers in the ear of one of the guards:

"It's the new man…"

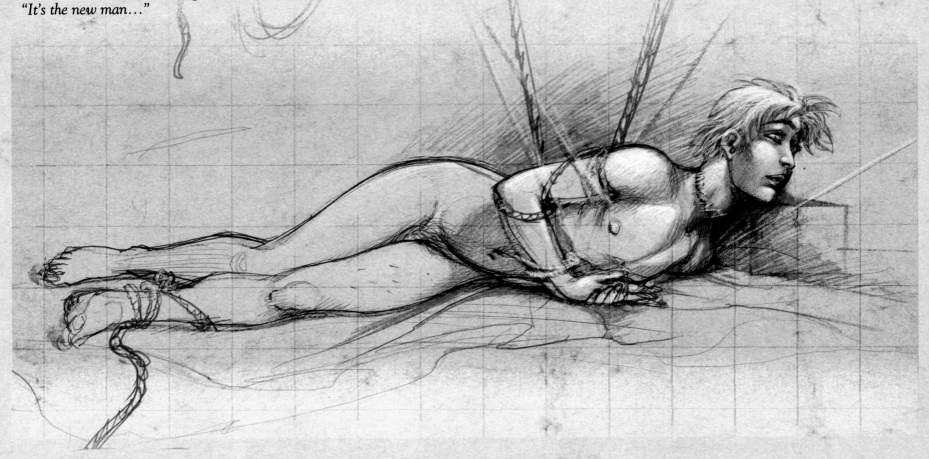

On the 8th of June of 1784, the festival of the Supreme Being takes place on the Champ de Mars. Atop several rocks, a statue has been raised. It has to embody, for several hours, that mystical, moral, and civic unanimity that Maximilien de Robespierre envisions for the future as a condition for peace and happiness.

AT FIRST, EVERYTHING WENT WELL.

YOU WERE WALKING AT THE HEAD, AS PLANNED, IN FRONT OF EVERYONE ELSE. THE STATUES OF ATHEISM AND NOTHING-NESS WERE BURNED, AS YOU WISHED.

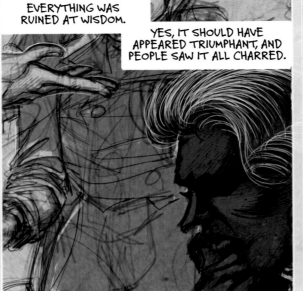

EVERYTHING WAS RUINED AT WISDOM.

YES, IT SHOULD HAVE APPEARED TRIUMPHANT, AND PEOPLE SAW IT ALL CHARRED.

THE CROWD COULD BE HEARD SNIGGERING. SOMEONE COULD HAVE SAID: THEIR WISDOM ISN'T LOOKING SO GOOD, IT HAS A BURNED SMELL.

PEOPLE WERE ALSO SAYING YOU WERE WALKING TOWARDS THE CAPITOL AND THAT YOUR FALL WASN'T FAR OFF.

SHUT UP!

NOBODY KNOWS WHAT THAT SUPREME BEING LOOKS LIKE. THE PEOPLE DON'T UNDERSTAND IT.

IF THE PEOPLE HAD AT LEAST SEEN AN IMAGE...

HOW DARE THEY?

IN THAT CASE, LET THEM SAVE THE REPUBLIC WITHOUT ME!

CALM YOURSELF, ROBESPIERRE, THERE WILL BE OTHER FESTIVALS.

YES, IN A FEW DAYS, THERE WILL BE THE ONE FOR BARA ON THE 10TH OF THERMI-DOR. EVERYTHING IS READY AND ORGANIZED. I'LL HAVE FINISHED HIS PORTRAIT!

WHICH ONE, DAVID?

THE ONE OF BARA. I ONLY HAVE THE BACKGROUND LEFT.

I ORDERED AN IMAGE OF THE SUPREME BEING FROM YOU, AND YOU'RE STILL LABORING AWAY AT THIS YOUNG BOY!

YOU BETRAYED ME!

CERTAINLY NOT! I DIDN'T SUCCEED IN PAINTING THAT SUPREME BEING, I'LL NEVER SUCCEED.

YOU'RE THE ONLY ONE WHO CAN IMAGINE HIM, MAXIMILIEN. AS YOU WELL KNOW, I'M ONLY A PAINTER, A CRAFTER.

HAVE YOU JOINED THE DISSIDENTS?

HOW DARE YOU SAY THAT?

MY ENEMIES ARE PLOTTING AGAINST ME, I KNOW. ARE YOU ONE OF THEM?

IF YOU HAVE ENEMIES, DENOUNCE THEM AT THE ASSEMBLY. NAME THEM! STARTING TOMORROW!

WHAT'S THE POINT, DAVID? I'M SO VERY TIRED. IF YOU ONLY KNEW...I THINK I'VE BEEN INVITED TO ANOTHER BANQUET, IN A NEW LIFE.

I JUST HAVE TO DRINK THE HEMLOCK.

IN THAT CASE, MAXIMILIEN, I'LL DRINK IT WITH YOU!

It's sweltering. At the Convention, everyone is waiting for Robespierre's speech, For him to name the dissidents, to point them out, and to name them enemies of the Revolution. The Terror claims new heads, and the supporters of the Incorruptible have gathered to back him. At a time when everyone trembles over their head, David refuses to leave his studio.

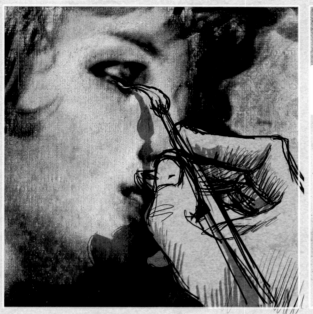

WHERE WERE YOU, DAVID? EVERYONE WAS EXPECTING YOU!

YOU SEE IT. I'M PAINTING. I'M FINISHING THE PORTRAIT OF BARA.

Serangeli appears, out of breath, in the deserted studio. In front of his painting, David is still applying himself, casting a look at his final sketches stuck to the wall, Jules' head sewn back on his body.

"*The Convention has voted to indict Robespierre. And along with him, Saint-Just, Couthon, and Lebas!!*"

The assistant is overwrought, his hand trembling. He cries:

"*The Revolution's in danger! The dissidents are rebelling! All our friends have taken shelter in the Hotêl de Ville and are calling out to the people…for an insurrection! QUICK! WE MUST FIGHT!*"

Without a word, David sets down his palette and takes a handkerchief. He blows his nose loudly.

"*Robespierre needs you! What are you waiting for to join him?*"

"*I have a terrible cold, can't you see?*"

"*A cold? In this heat?*" repeats Serangeli, not understanding.

"*Yes…pass me that vial there on the chair. I'm going to drink some emetic.*"

Dumbfounded, the assistant passes the designated vial to him. David drinks it in one gulp.

Robespierre and his supporters are arrested on the 8th of Thermidor and

guillotined the next day. Three days later, David is imprisoned. In a letter addressed to his accusers, he denounces the tyranny of the Incorruptible, disavows his former convictions, and thus, no doubt, saves his head. The festival in honor of the young Bara, planned for the 10th of Thermidor, doesn't take place. His portrait remains unfinished.

There never was a painting of the Supreme Being.

Three years later, David is amnestied. He returns to his studio in the Louvre, "which he ought to have never left." He proposes to General Bonaparte to do his portrait. Hurried, as was his wont, the hero of the Italian campaign grants him a fifteen-minute pose. Scarcely has the general departed when David confides his enthusiasm to his students.

WHAT A HEAD HE HAS! HIS LOOK TURNED TOWARDS THE SUMMITS, TOWARDS THE BEYOND.

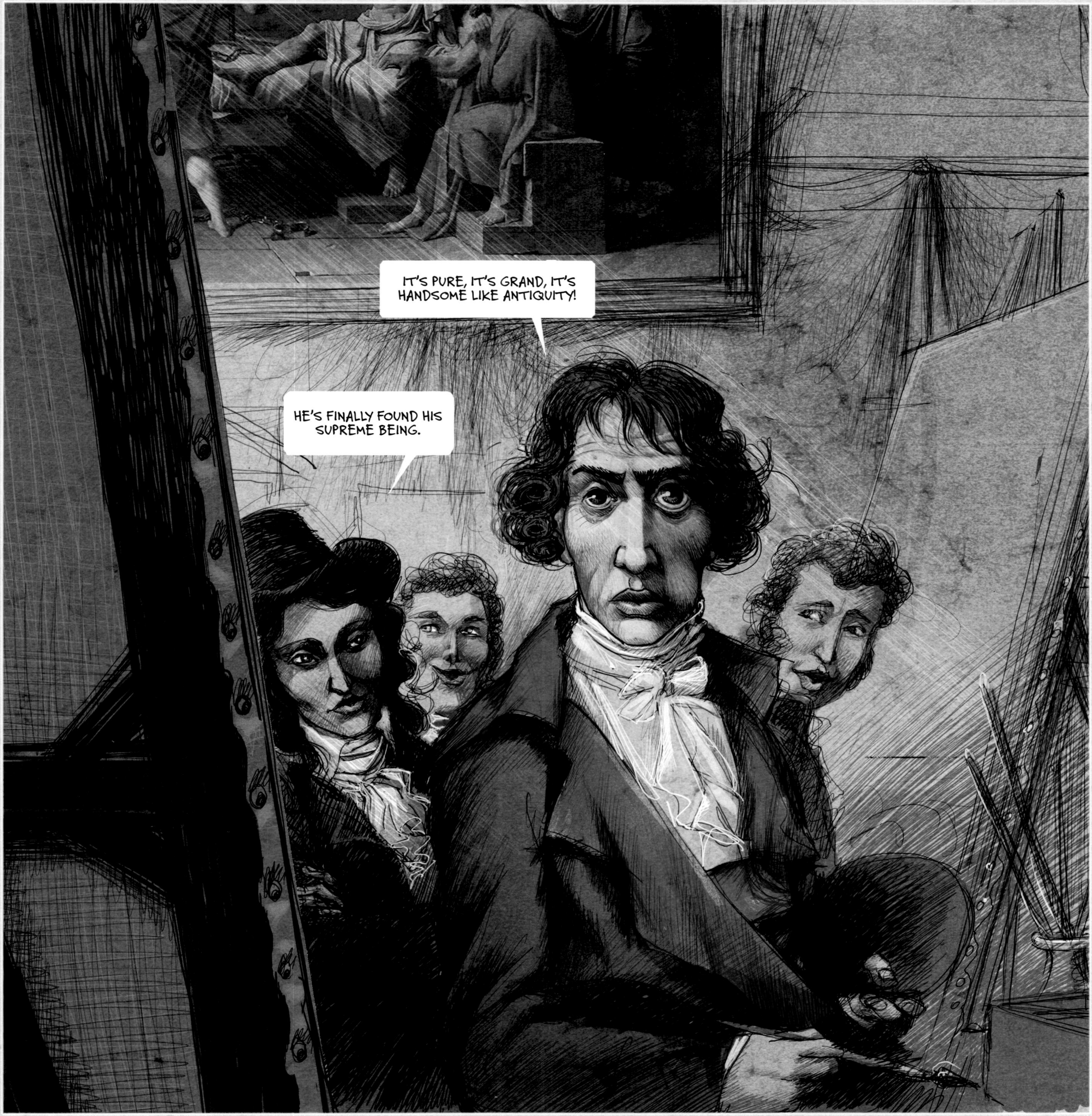
IT'S PURE, IT'S GRAND, IT'S HANDSOME LIKE ANTIQUITY!
HE'S FINALLY FOUND HIS SUPREME BEING.

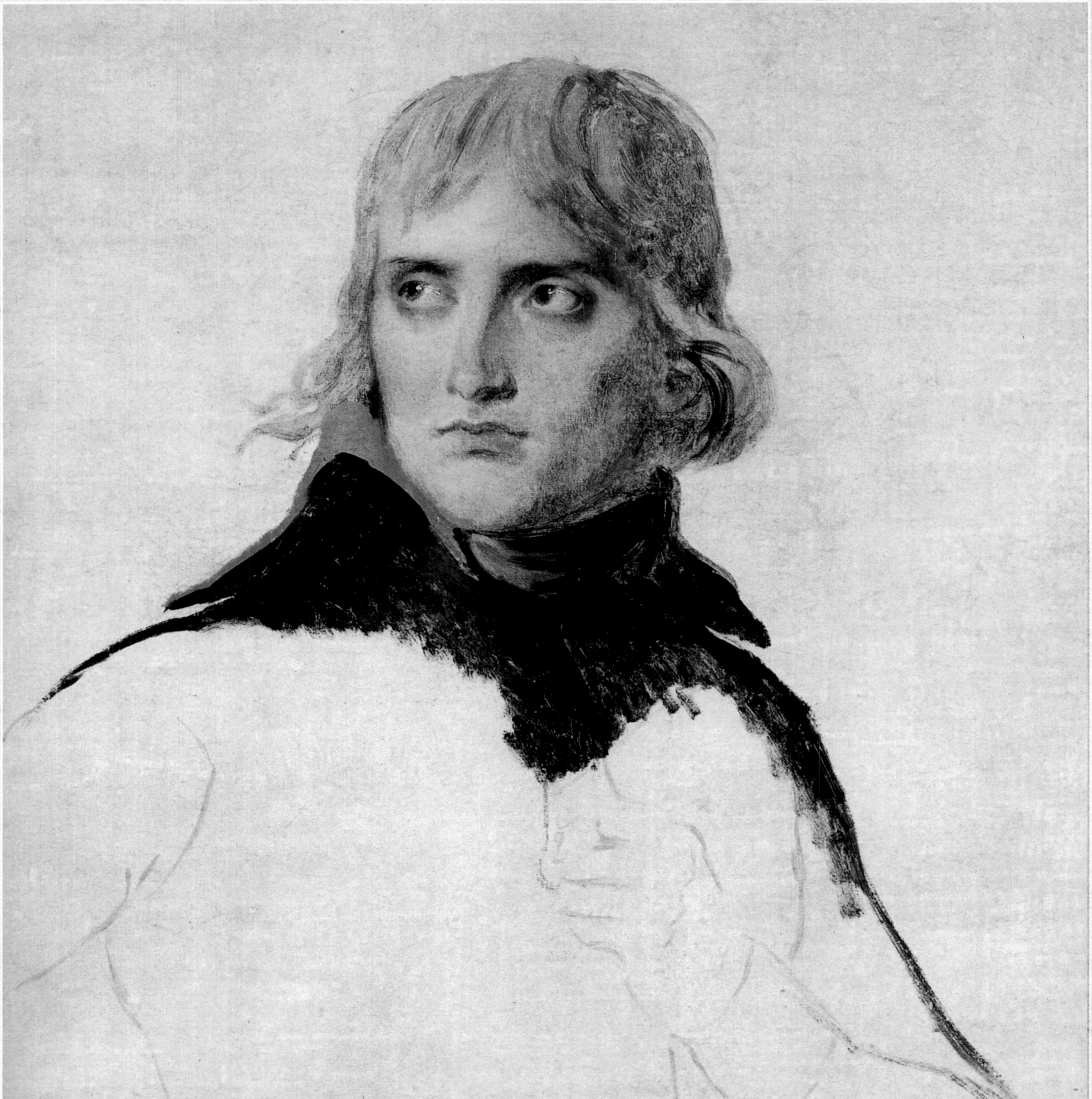

Appendices

List of works chosen by the author, in order of appearance.

Unless indicated otherwise, all of the works reproduced in this volume are in the collections of the Musée du Louvre. Some works were not yet part of the Louvre's collections at the time of the events related and were acquired later. Some of them have never been part of the collections. We have indicated their provenance as needed.

PAGES 4, 5, 30, AND 31
Jacques-Louis David
Marat Assassinated, 1793
Oil on canvas, H: 1.65 m x W: 1.28 m.
Brussels, Musées royaux des Beaux-Arts of Belgium
© MRBAB/KMSKB (Photo Cussac)

PAGE 12
Vecellio Tiziano, known as Titian
Woman With a Mirror, circa 1515
Oil on canvas, H: 99 cm x W. 89 cm; INV 755
Denon, 1st Floor, Salle de la Joconde, room 7.

Vecellio Tiziano, known as Titian
Portrait of a Man, known as "Man with a Glove" circa 1520
Oil on canvas, H: 1 m x W: 89 cm; INV 757
Louis XIV Collection, acquired from Jabach in 1671,
Denon, salle des États

Georges de la Tour
The Cheat with the Ace of Diamonds, 1635
Oil on canvas, H: 1.06 m x W: 1.46 m; RF 1972
Sully, 2nd floor, room 28

Lucas van Valckenburgh
The Tower of Babel, 1594
Oil on wood, H: 41 cm x W: 56 cm; RF 2427
Richelieu, 2nd Floor, room 13

Jean Baptiste Siméon Chardin
The Bird-Organ, 1751
Oil on canvas, H: 50 cm x W: 43 cm; RF 1985-10
Sully, 2nd Floor, room 40

Aelbrecht Cuyp
Landscape near Rhenen: cows in the pasture and shepherd playing the flute, 1650-1655
Oil on canvas, H: 1.70 m x W: 2.29 m; INV. 1190
Louis XVI Collection: acquired in Brussels, 1783
Richelieu, 2nd floor, room 34

Frans Hals
The Gypsy Girl, circa 1626
Oil on canvas, H: 58 cm x W: 52 cm; M.I. 926
Bequest of Dr. Louis La Caze (1798-1869), 1869
Richelieu, 2nd Floor, room 28

Bartolomé Esteban Murillo
The Young Beggar, circa 1645-1650
Oil on canvas, H: 1.34 m x W:1.10 m; INV. 933
Louis XVI Collection (acquired in 1782)

Jean-Siméon Chardin
Grace
Oil on canvas, H: 49 cm x W: 38 cm; INV 3202-Salon of 1740
Louis XV Collection, given by the artist to the king in 1740;
Sully, 2nd Floor, room 40

Paolo Caliari, known as Veronese
The Wedding Feast at Cana, 1563
Oil on canvas, H: 6.77 m x W: 9.94 m; INV. 142
Completed in 1563 for the refectory of the Benedictines of San Giorgio Maggiore in Venice, entered the Louvre in 1798.
Denon, 1st Floor, salle des États, room 6

Jean-Honoré Fragonard
The Bolt, circa 1777
Oil on canvas, H: 74 cm x W: 94 cm; RF 1974-2
Acquired in 1974
Sully, 2nd Floor, room 48

Leonardo di ser Piero Da Vinci, known as Leonardo da Vinci
Portrait of Lisa Gherardini, wife of Francesco del Giocondo, known as The Mona Lisa, The Gioconda, or The Joconde, Circa 1503-1506
Oil on wood (poplar), H: 77 cm x W: 53 cm.; INV. 779
Acquired by Francis 1st in 1518
Denon, 1st Floor, La Joconde room

Jean Clouet
Portrait of Francis 1st, King of France, circa 1530
Oil on wood, H: 96 cm x W: 74 cm; INV. 3256
Collection of Francis 1st
Richelieu, 2nd Floor, room 7

Albrecht Dürer
Portrait of the Artist Holding a Thistle, 1493
H: 56 cm x W: 44cm; RF 2382
Richelieu, 2nd Floor, room 8

Georges de la Tour
The Penitent Magdalene, Circa 1640-1645
H: 1.28 m x W: 94 cm, RF 1949-11
Acquired in 1949
Sully, 2nd Floor, room 28

Charles Le Brun
Chancellor Séguier at the Entry of Louis XIV into Paris in 1660, circa 1655-1661
H: 2.95 m x W: 3.57 m, RF 1972-14
Acquired from the model's descendants, with the support of the association Friends of the Louvre, 1942
Sully, 2nd Floor, room 31

Jean-Honoré Fragonard
Denis Diderot, circa 1769
H: 82 cm x W: 65 cm; RF 1972-14
Acquired by gift in 1972
Sully, 2nd Floor, room 48

PAGES 12 AND 14
François Boucher
Diana Leaving Her Bath, 1742
H: 57 cm x W: 73 cm; Inv
Acquired in 1852
Sully, 2nd Floor, room 38

PAGES 13 AND 25
Anne-Louis Girodet de Roussy-Trioson
Endymion. Moonlight Effect, also known as The Sleep of Endymion.
H: 1.98 m x W: 2.61 m; INV. 4935
Salons of 1793 and 1814
Denon, 1st Floor, Daru, room 75
© RMN/René-Gabriel Ojéda

PAGE 13
François Xavier Fabre
The Death of Abel
Montpellier, Musée Fabre, INV. 825.1.60
© Musée Fabre, Montpellier Agglomeration

PAGES 13, 14, 33, ET 36
Jacques-Louis David
Académie d'homme, known as Hector, 1778
Oil on canvas, H: 1.23 m x W: 1.72 m
Montpellier, Musée Fabre, INV. 851-1-1
© RMN/ Rights Reserved

PAGE 14
Jacques-Louis David
Académie d'homme, known as Patroclus, 1780
Oil on canvas, H: 1.22 m x W: 1.70 m
Cherbourg, Musée Thomas Henry, INV. 835.102

Guido Reni
Hercules Overcoming the Lernaean Hydra, 1617-1621
Oil on canvas, H: 2.60 m x W: 1.92 m; INV. 535
Louis XIV Collection (acquired in 1662)
Denon, 1st Floor, Grand Gallery, room 12

Guido Reni
Hercules on the Pyre, 1617-1619
Oil on canvas, H: 2.60 m x W: 1.92 m; INV. 538
Louis XIV Collection (acquired in 1662)
Denon, 1st Floor, Grand Gallery, room 12

François Boucher
Diana Leaving Her Bath, 1742
Oil on canvas, H: 57 cm x W: 73 cm; INV. 2712
Sully, 2nd Floor, room 38

PAGES 14, 24, 33, AND 35
Jacques-Louis David
The Oath of the Horatii, 1784
Oil on canvas, H: 3.30 m x W: 4.25 m; INV. 3692
Louis XVI Collection
Denon, 1st Floor, Daru, room 75

PAGE 15
Michelangelo Buonarroti, known as Michelangelo
Captive ("The Dying Slave")
Marble, H: 2.28 m, M.R. 1590, executed In 1513-1515 for the tomb of Pope Julius II.
Denon, Ground Floor, Michelangelo Gallery, room 4

Apollo of Smyrna of the type of the *Lycian Apollo*, known as *Bacchus* Circa 130-150 A.D. (?) after an original created in the second half of the IV century B.C. (?)
Pentelic Marble, H. 216 cm inventory number MR 79, ordinary number Ma 928
Seizure by the Revolution, 1798
Department of Greek, Etruscan, and Roman Antiquities.

Lambert-Sigisbert Adam
Neptune Calming the Waves
Marble, H: 85 cm; W: 59 cm; D: 48 cm, Inv. M.R. 1743
Reception piece at the Academy, 1737
Seizure by the Revolution of the Collections of the Academy
Richelieu, Ground floor, The Small Gallery of the Academy, room 25

PAGE 25 AND 26
Jacques-Louis David
Madame Charles-Louis Trudaine, 1791-1792
H: 1.30 m x W: 98 cm; R.F. 690
Sully, 2nd Floor, David and his students, room 54

PAGE 30
Reconstitution of *Lepeletier de Saint-Fargeau on his deathbed (1793)*,
After a drawing of A. Devosge (Dijon, Musée des Beaux-Arts)
Original work of Jacques-Louis David, missing since 1826

PAGE 36 AND 63
Jacques-Louis David
The Death of Socrates, 1787
Oil on canvas, H: 1.29 m x W: 1.96 m; Catharine Lorillard Wolfe Collection, Wolfe Fund, 1931 (31.45)
New York, The Metropolitan Museum of Art, INV. 31.45

PAGES 43, 44, 60, 61, 62, AND 63
Jacques-Louis David
Death of Joseph Bara
Oil on canvas, H: 1.18 m x W: 1.55 m
Avignon, Musée Calvet, INV. 146

PAGE 64
Jacques-Louis David
Pierre Sériziat, brother-in-law of the artist (1757–1847)
Salon of 1795
Oil on wood, H. 1.29 m; W: 95 cm; RF 1281
Denon, 1st Floor, Daru, room 75

Jacques-Louis David
Madame Pierre Sériziat, sister of Mrs. David, and one of her sons, Émile, born in 1793, known as Portrait of Émilie Sériziat and Her Son, 1793
Salon of 1795
Oil on wood, H: 1.31 m x W: 96 cm; RF 1282
Denon, 1st Floor, Daru, room 75

Jacques-Louis David
Preparatory Drawing for The Intervention of the Sabine Women, circa 1799
Black chalk, pen and black ink, Gray wash with white heightening, on brown paper
H: 25.6 cm x W: 35.9 cm; inv. RF 5200
Department of Graphic Arts

PAGE 66
Jacques-Louis David
General Bonaparte, Circa 1797-1798
Oil on canva (sketch)
H: 81 cm x W: 65 cm; RF 1942-18
Sully 2nd Floor, room A
© RMN/René-Gabriel Ojéda

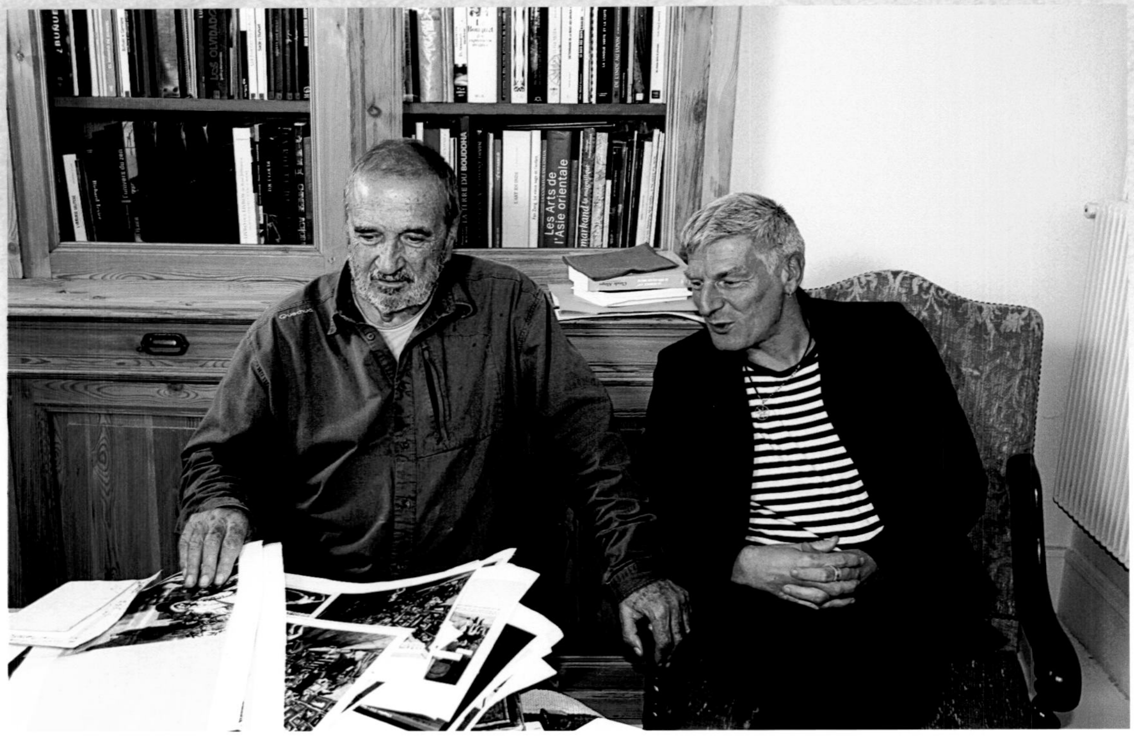
Les Arts de
l'Asie orientale

Bernar Yslaire

Born Bernard Hislaire, January 11, 1957 in Brussels.

He starts his comics career with a children's comic in Spirou magazine, *Bidouille et Violette* in 1978.

In 1986 he launches his most famous oeuvre, *Sambre*, a Romanesque historic fresco that has sold in the millions of copies in many languages.

He becomes one of the first comic artists to embrace the internet with the online creation of *Memories of the XXth Sky*, a story in the fantastic genre.

In 2006, he publishes *Sky Over Brussels*, a story of a European man falling for a lovely muslim woman, whom he finds out is to be a suicide bomber.

After a long hiatus, he comes back to *Sambre* in 2007 but only as the writer.

January 2009: he exhibits at the Musée du Louvre a video of his technique on this book 'in real time.'

May 2009: he is anointed Chevalier of Arts & Letters by the French minister of culture.

Jean-Claude Carrière

Born September 17, 1931 in France.

After a first novel in 1957, he begins a long career in screenwriting.

Notably, he works with Buñuel for 19 years until the director's death. This includes such films as *Belle de Jour* (1967), *The Discreet Charm of the Bourgeoisie* (1972), *The Phantom of Liberty* (1974), *That Obscure Object of Desire* (1977) and *The Milky Way* (1969).

He also does scripts for such directors as Louis Malle, Milos Forman and adaptations of *Cyrano de Bergerac*, *The Tin Drum*, and *The Unbearable Lightness of Being*.

This is not the first time Carrière has tackled the subject of the French revolution: he also wrote the screenplay for Andrzej Wajda's *Danton*.

He is as well the author of numerous novels and books.

This is his first script for a graphic novel.

Musée du Louvre

Henri Loyrette
President and Director

Hervé Barbaret
General Administrator

Catherine Sueur
Assistant General Administrator

Juliette Armand
Head of Cultural Development

Violaine Bouvet-Lanselle
Head of the Publishing Service, Office of Cultural Development

Publishing

Series Editor
Fabrice Douar
Publishing Service, Office of Cultural Development, Musée du Louvre

Acknowledgments at the Musée du Louvre

Henri Loyrette, Hervé Barbaret, Catherine Sueur, Juliette Armand,
Régis Michel, Marie-Catherine Sahut, Guillaume Fonkenell,
Pascal Torrès, Carole Grandisson, Anna di Pietra, Christel Winling,
Lucia Marabini, Nelly Girault, Chrystel Martin, Virginie Fabre,
Violaine Bouvet-Lanselle, Fanny Meurisse, Diane Vernel, Adrien Goetz,
Laurence Castany, Catherine Dupont, Christine Fuzeau, Camille Sourisse,
Aurélia Cimelière, Soraya Karkache, Sixtine de Saint-Léger, Laurence Petit,
Véronique Petitjean, Zahia Chettab, Nathalie Brac de La Perrière.

Thanks to Carole de Vellou, Catherine Lamarre, Lina Propeck, Jean Galard,
Charlotte Lacombe, Michel Nicolas, Moïna Lisowski, Pascal Bequet,
Thierry Masbou, Georges Rubel, Aline Sylla-Walbaum
for their invaluable support.

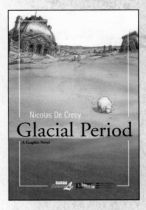

ComicsLit is an imprint
and trademark of

NANTIER • BEALL • MINOUSTCHINE
Publishing inc.
new york